Disney · PIXAR

ANNUAL 2009

EGMONT

We bring stories to life

First published in Great Britain in 2008
by Egmont UK Limited
239 Kensington High Street, London W8 6SA

Editor: Jaine Keskeys
Art Editor: Phil Williams

ISBN 978 1 4052 3901 1
1 3 5 7 9 10 8 6 4 2
Printed in Italy

This annual belongs to

Name:

....

Age:

....

My favourite character is:

....

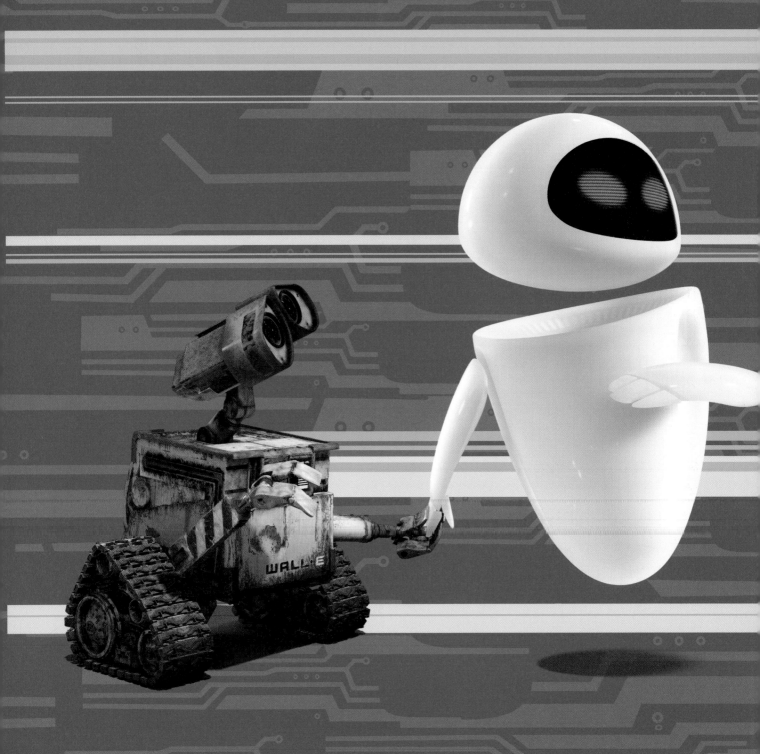

Disney · PIXAR
WALL·E

Disney · PIXAR
RATATOUILLE
(rat·a·too·ee)

Disney · PIXAR
THE WORLD OF Cars

Disney · PIXAR
FINDING NEMO

Disney · PIXAR
THE INCREDIBLES

Disney · PIXAR
TOY STORY AND BEYOND!

Disney · PIXAR
MONSTERS, INC.

New friends

1. Every day, a lonely little robot called WALL·E collected up the rubbish that had ruined Earth. Humans now lived in space, on a huge spaceship.

2. WALL·E took home many treasures he found in the rubbish and one day he found a plant. WALL·E didn't know what it was, but he knew it was special.

3. Suddenly, there was a huge sand storm, caused by a spaceship landing on Earth! WALL·E watched as a white probe-bot appeared from the ship.

4. The probe-bot was called EVE and WALL·E was soon showing his new friend around his home. EVE loved seeing the treasures WALL·E had found!

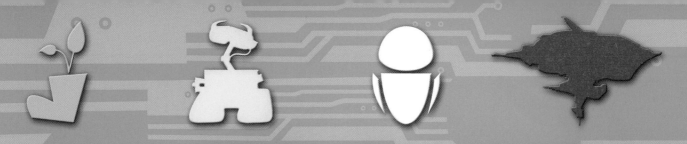

5. When WALL·E showed EVE the plant, something strange happened. EVE's front opened up and she put the plant inside her. Then, she shut down.

6. Soon, the spaceship returned to collect EVE. WALL·E wanted to stay with EVE, so he followed her aboard. It flew into space with WALL·E inside!

7. WALL·E had known the plant was special, but in space he discovered that it could save Earth! WALL·E and EVE worked together to keep the plant safe.

8. After their space adventure, WALL·E and EVE returned to Earth. Saving the planet was a tough job for a little robot and WALL·E needed some repairs!

9. Soon, WALL·E was as good as new. And so was Earth! Humans would return, now that plants could grow there once again.

10. Best of all, WALL·E had some new friends. He'd met more robots on the spaceship and was no longer a lonely little robot living on a deserted planet!

The end

About the story

1 What special treasure did WALL·E find?

2 What was the white probe-bot called?

3 Where did EVE put the plant?

4 Who needed some repairs?

10

Answers: 1. A plant. 2. EVE. 3. Inside herself. 4. WALL·E.

Clean-up changes

Can you find the 6 differences in the bottom picture of WALL·E? Colour Earth each time you spot one.

Hanging around

Stick this page on to card and then cut out the hanger. Fold it over and glue the backs together. Now it's ready to hang on your door!

Fold here

© Disney/Pixar

© Disney/Pixar

Keep my room tidy!

WALL·E
WASTE ALLOCATION LOAD LIFTER – EARTH CLASS

THIS IS MY SPACE!

Disney · PIXAR

WALL·E

Fold here

Parts puzzle

WALL·E is busy cleaning planet Earth. Which six circles show parts of WALL·E?

Scanning shades

EVE is scanning for something. Add some colours to help her search!

Match-up M-O

Can you put these pictures of M-O into matching pairs? Draw a line to join each pair together!

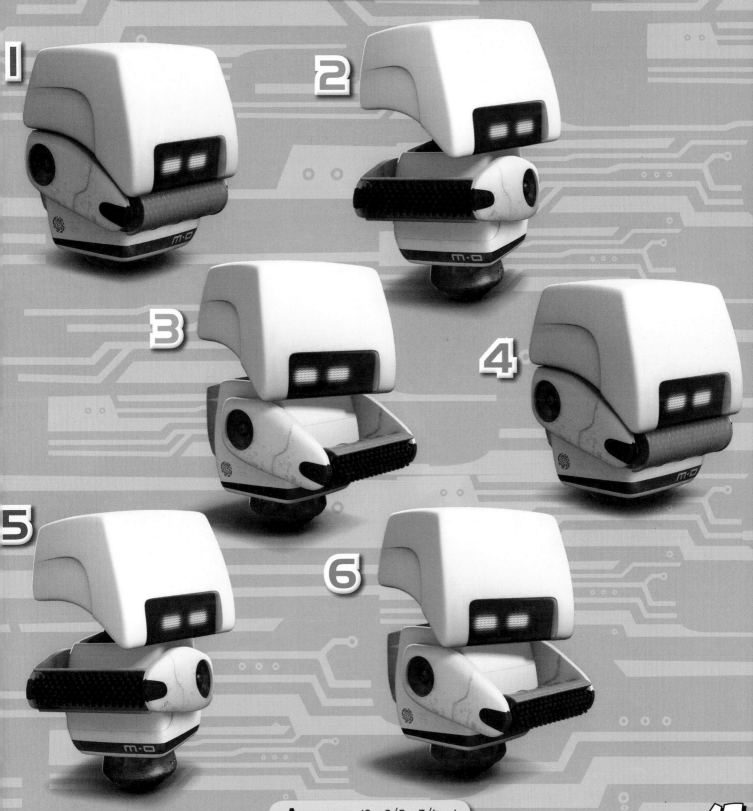

Space race

Join WALL·E and race around space in this great game!

You will need: A dice, two counters and a pen.

Player card 1

Start

1

2

18

17

16

15

14

13

12

How to play

This is a game for two players. Choose a player card each, then take it in turns to roll the dice and move your counter around and around the board. If you land on a space object, tick the matching box on your player card. The first player to tick all of their boxes is the winner!

Player card 2

Which one?

Can you spot which one is the odd picture out in each row?

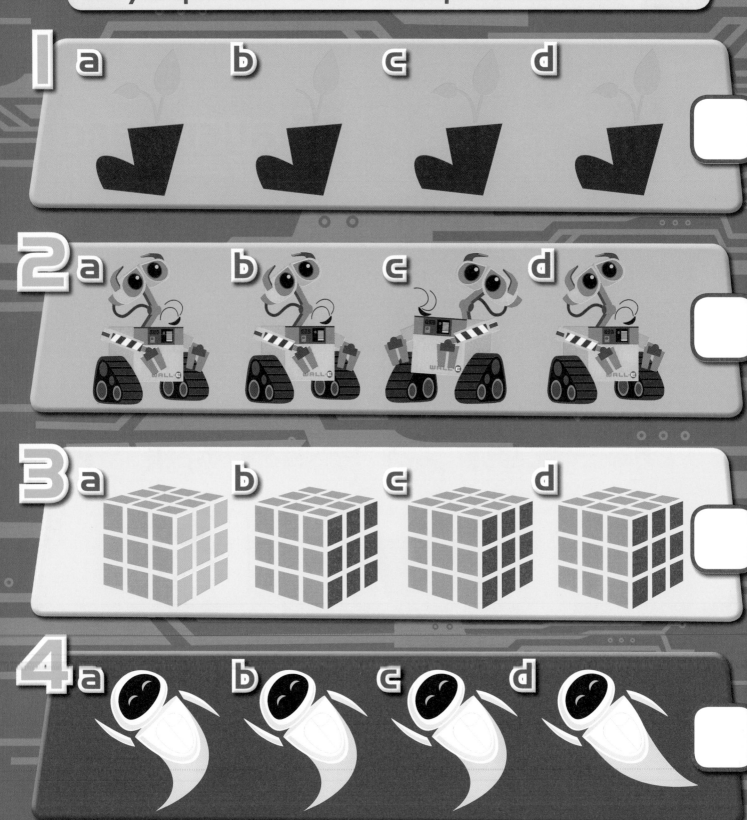

1 a b c d

2 a b c d

3 a b c d

4 a b c d

18

Answer: 1-b, 2-c, 3-a, 4-d.

WALL·E and EVE

Give WALL·E and his friend EVE some happy colours!

Quick chef

1. La Ratatouille was the most popular restaurant in Paris! Linguini had given the waiters roller-skates, so that they could race around and take orders.

2. "We've never been so busy!" Ego said, as Linguini skated past him. More customers arrived every day, wanting to be served by the speedy waiters!

3. "I don't know how Remy manages to cook so many meals at once," Ego said. "I've got something that will make it easier for him!" Linguini replied.

4. In the kitchen, Remy was rushed off his little feet. Pans were starting to boil over and there was a smell of burning food. "I can't keep up!" Remy panted.

5. Linguini knew that there were too many orders now for one little chef! "You can't cook as fast as the waiters can serve," Linguini said.

6. "Don't worry, Little Chef," Linguini told his friend. "I have something to help you." He handed Remy a pair of tiny, red roller-skates, just like his!

7. Remy was so excited! He put on his new roller-skates and raced around the kitchen. Now, it was easy for him to cook all the food!

8. With his new wheels, Remy was a very fast rat. "Now the waiters are going to have trouble keeping up with me!" Remy thought, happily.

The end

21

Tower power

Remy has built three cheese towers! Can you put them in order, starting with the tallest tower?

a

b

c

Which tower has five pieces of cheese? Write your answer in the box.

Finger puppets

Here's how to make some little rat finger puppets. Remy loves them!

You will need: Blue card, pink card, glue, scissors, pink wool, a black marker pen and googly eyes.

1 Cut out a circle of blue card. Cut a triangle from it and then bend it into a cone and glue it in place.

Use brown card to make Emile, too!

2 Cut out ears from the pink card and cut a length of pink wool for a tail and stick them on. Draw on a nose and stick on googly eyes!

23

Kitchen capers

It's chaos in the kitchen! Help Linguini and Colette get things back on track by answering these tasty teasers!

1 What is Colette chopping up?

2 What word is in the frying pan?

3 Where is Remy, the rat?

Food fun

What tasty colours will you use to colour Emile's sneaky snack?

Can you spot a banana skin somewhere in the picture? Tick the box when you find it.

Odd one out

This page is making Emile's mouth water! Can you spot the odd one out in each row?

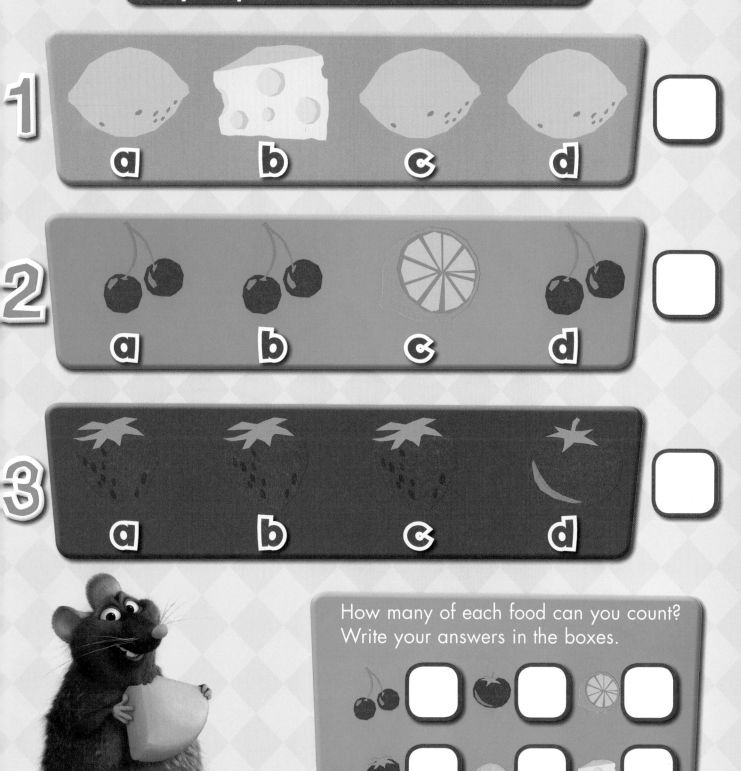

How many of each food can you count? Write your answers in the boxes.

Food fight!

Remy and Emile are having a food fight. Why don't you join them for some messy fun!

You will need: Coloured pens and a dice.

2

3

4

1

5

6

Remy

How to play

Decide which rat each player will be and then take it in turns to throw the dice. Colour in the food splat that matches the number you have thrown. Miss a go if that food splat is already coloured. The first player to colour in all their food splats wins the food fight!

3

4

2

5

1

6

Emile

A sandy solution

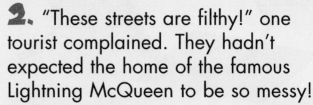

1. One day, a strong wind storm blew through Radiator Springs. Sand was blowing all over Main Street and the tourists were very disappointed.

2. "These streets are filthy!" one tourist complained. They hadn't expected the home of the famous Lightning McQueen to be so messy!

3. Red, Ramone and Mater had overheard the tourists' comments. "We can't have this. Let's clean this sand up, right now!" said Ramone.

4. The friends worked hard to clear the sand into a pile, but the tourists still weren't happy. "I wanted to see Lightning McQueen," they grumbled.

5. "Don't worry, I have an idea," Ramone told the tourists. He told Red and Mater what to do and, together, they put his plan into action.

6. As soon as Red and Mater were finished, Ramone used his paint nozzle. "Perfect!" he laughed. "There shouldn't be any more complaints!"

7. "Now, everyone will know they've come to the right town," said Mater, admiring his work. The sand pile looked just like Lightning McQueen!

8. When the tourists saw the sand car, they thought it was really great! Lightning McQueen thought so, too. "Great job, guys!" he laughed.

The end

Movie night

The cars in Radiator Springs are enjoying an exciting movie!
Can you answer these questions before the film is finished?

1 Can you spot the popcorn in the picture?

2 Can you spot Sally, the blue porsche?

3 How many cars are watching the movie?

Answers: 1. The popcorn is beside the orange car. 2. Sally is between Mater and McQueen. 3. 6 cars are watching the movie.

McQueen's cones

What does McQueen like doing best? Follow the road and as you pass the cones, copy the letters into the boxes at the bottom.

Copy the letters into the boxes!

Answer: McQueen likes racing.

Hanging out

Lightning McQueen and Sally are chilling out with Fillmore!

1 Can you find this flower on Fillmore's tent?

2 What word is written on Fillmore?

3 Which of these sculptures does not appear in the main picture?

a b c d

4 Which of these barrels is not one of a matching pair?

5 Colour in McQueen!

6 How many oil cans can you count?

35

Mud splats

Racing around has made these cars muddy! Can you answer the questions before they get cleaned up?

1 Which car has the most mud splats?

Sheriff

Fillmore

Doc

McQueen

2 Which car has no mud splats?

Sally

3 What colour do the splats on Sally need to be to disappear?

Answers: 1. McQueen has the most mud splats. 2. Sheriff has no mud splats. 3. The splats on Sally need to be blue to disappear.

36

Drive time

Make Sally and McQueen's drive more colourful!

37

Unseen attack

1. One day, Marlin and Dory were swimming in a shallow part of the ocean when they came across a shoal of fish, hiding in some seaweed.

2. "Hi, guys! What are you all doing in there? The water out here's lovely," said Marlin. "It's far too scary to come out," replied one of the fish.

3. Marlin and Dory looked around, but they couldn't see anything scary. Suddenly, snapping beaks came diving down at them. "Seagulls!" cried Marlin.

4. "Seagulls fly just above the water. We never know when they're going to attack!" explained the fish, as Marlin and Dory joined them in the seaweed.

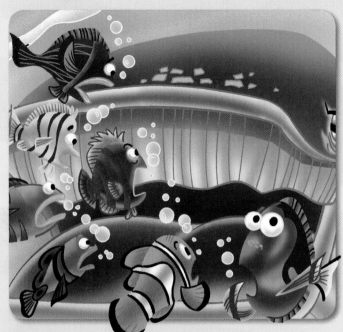

5. Dory suggested that they should swim in a deeper part of the ocean. "Aren't there dangerous things down there, too?" gulped the nervous fish.

6. "Nah!" giggled Dory, just as a huge mouth opened up in front of them. "Oh, I forgot about the whales! They don't like to be disturbed," she said.

7. "Luckily I can speak whale!" Dory chuckled, making silly sounds. And to Marlin's surprise, the whales followed Dory to the shallow water.

8. "Now!" Dory cried. The whales blasted water from their spouts high into the air, soaking the screeching seagulls. "They won't be back!" laughed Dory.

The end **39**

Marlin's mates

Give Marlin and his sea turtle friends some fun colours!

Nemo's shells

Nemo and his friends have found some colourful shells. Can you complete the sequences below, by colouring the white shells the correct colours?

1

2

3

4

Fish are friends

Join the meeting and share some fun with Marlin, Dory and the hungry sharks.

1 What has Chum just eaten?

Anchor

2 Who is raising their fin to speak – Dory or Marlin?

Chum

Dory

3 Which detail below does not appear in the main picture?

a   b   c   d   e

Reef race

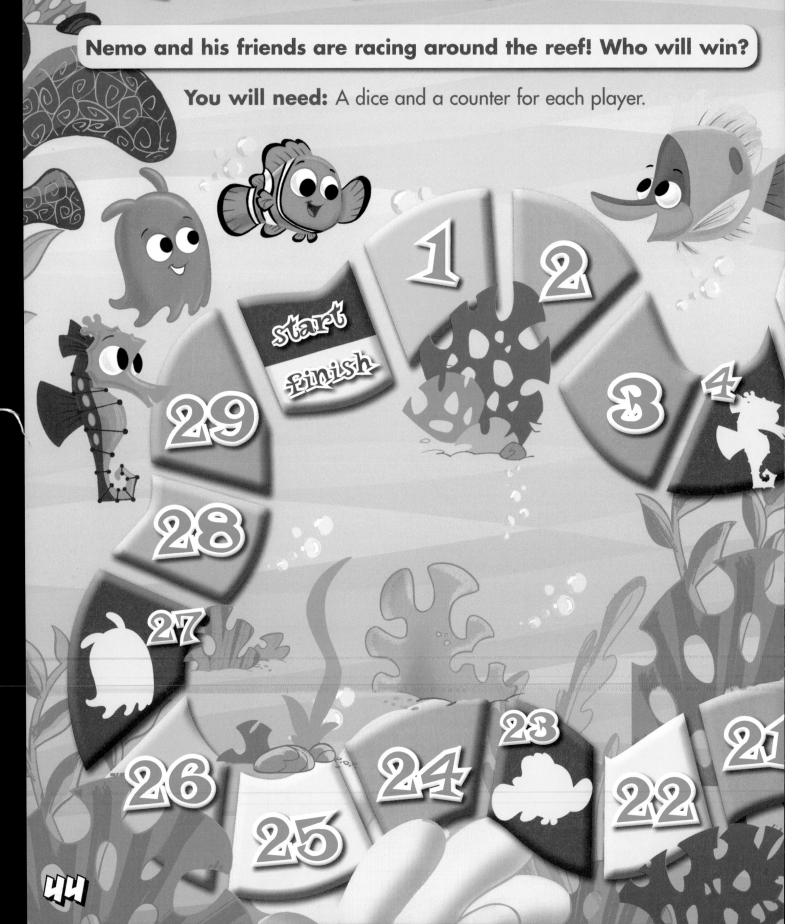

Nemo and his friends are racing around the reef! Who will win?

You will need: A dice and a counter for each player.

Start
Finish

1
2
3
4
29
28
27
26
25
24
23
22
21

How to play

Decide which character each player will be – Nemo, Sheldon, Tad or Pearl. Place all the counters on the start/finish space and take it in turns to roll the dice and move around the path. If you land on a space that contains your character's shadow, have an extra turn. But if you land on a space that contains another character's shadow, miss a turn. The first player to reach the start/finish space again is the winner!

45

Draw Dory

Finish this picture of Dory and add some stinging colours!

Fish finder

Which two fish from the top picture swam away and don't appear in the bottom picture?

Answer: The pink fish with the pink stripes and the blue fish with the teeth.

47

Super suits

1. One day, the Incredible family went to Edna Mode's laboratory, to collect their Super suits. "They are inside my latest creation," E told them, proudly.

2. E quickly ushered them inside the Mega Transformation Hyper Conduction Pod and pressed a button. "Change commencing," boomed the machine.

3. However, when they emerged, something wasn't right. Mr. Incredible's suit was made of Super stretchy material. It was so tight that he could hardly walk!

4. Meanwhile, Violet came out of the machine in a very short suit. "I know I'm growing tall pretty quickly, but this is ridiculous!" she gasped in surprise.

5. Dash laughed when he saw Violet, but he soon stopped giggling when the suit he was wearing became invisible! He dashed to hide behind a plant.

6. Elastigirl was wearing a big, baggy suit. "I don't think your new machine is working too well, E. It's given each of us the wrong suit!" she chuckled.

7. So E re-checked the control panel. "Darling, the machine is perfect. The mistake is mine. I put the suits on the wrong hangers!" she giggled.

8. E soon fixed the mix-up. When the Incredibles went back into the machine, they came out wearing their own suits. "That's Super, E!" they cheered.

The end!

A Super battle

Can you defeat these questions faster than the Incredibles can defeat this Omnidroid?

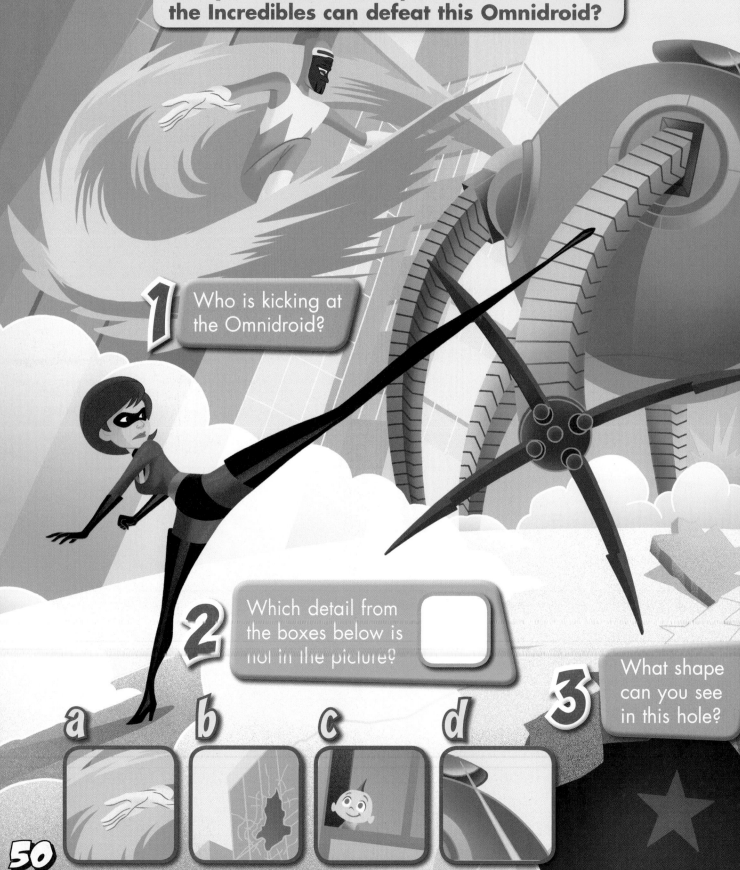

1 Who is kicking at the Omnidroid?

2 Which detail from the boxes below is not in the picture?

3 What shape can you see in this hole?

a   b   c   d

4 How many holes has the Omnidroid made in the blue building?

5 What weighty word is written below?

heavy

a

b

c

d

e

6 Which two chunks of pavement look the same?

Answers: 1. Elastigirl. 2. Detail c. 3. A star shape. 4. 3. 5. heavy 6. Chunks a and c.

51

On the button

Mr. Incredible knows the password is KRONOS but which colour button has all the correct letters? Follow the path to see if you're right.

KRONOS

Answer: The red button.

Cool maze

Can you guide Frozone through this maze? Answer any questions you run into on route!

Start ➡

1 Rearrange the letters on Frozone's ice disk, to find a cool word.

2 Who is Frozone's Super best friend?

3 These three words all end in the word ice. Can you complete them?

n ⬜ ⬜ ⬜
m ⬜ ⬜ ⬜
tw ⬜ ⬜ ⬜

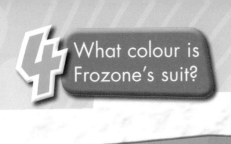

4 What colour is Frozone's suit?

5 Which of the phrases below would Frozone say?

a "Gotta disappear!"

b "Freeze!"

c "Stretched to my limits!"

6 What is ice made from?

Finish

Buzz's story

1. One day, Buzz was telling Rex about his adventures. "With my anti-gravity boots, I can run up rocks," he said, pointing to the notice board.

2. "Anti-gravity boots! You don't actually believe that story do you, Rex?" laughed Woody. "Buzz doesn't really have anti-gravity boots!"

3. "I'll show you," said Buzz. He looked around and saw a clear bit of wall, next to the window. He ran fast and went straight up the wall.

4. But Buzz only got a little way up before he fell. He tried to grab the curtain but he tumbled out of the open window. The toys all gasped in horror.

5. Woody and Rex raced to the window and looked out. Buzz had landed safely in a rubbish bin, below. But how would he get back up?

6. "This is all my fault. I've got to help Buzz!" cried Woody. Suddenly, he remembered the notice board. "It'll be just like Buzz's story!" he cheered.

7. So, Woody threw two magnets and some sticky tape down to Buzz. "Strap on your new anti-gravity boots!" Woody yelled to his friend.

8. Buzz did as Woody said. Then he walked up the metal drainpipe. "That's amazing!" gasped Rex. "I love my new anti-gravity boots!" giggled Buzz.

The end

Drawing time

Draw a picture on the screen, then colour in the scene!

58

Brick by brick

Can you work out how many bricks each character needs to complete their wall?

Woody

Rex

Buzz

Jessie

Answer: Woody – 8, Rex – 6, Buzz – 5, Jessie – 7.

A big bounce

Can you answer these questions before Buzz Lightyear lands?

1 Who is up on the bed with Slinky?

2 Where is the orange star?

3 Who is hiding under the bed?

4 What colour is the car doing the loop?

5 How many cars can you count?

6 Where do you think Buzz will land?

Answers: 1. Woody. 2. On the ball. 3. Rex. 4. Green. 5. 4. 6. Buzz will land on the bed.

61

The lost tickets

1. One evening, Mike was very excited. "I've got tickets to the newest club in Monstropolis!" he told Sulley. "I'm meeting Celia there in an hour!"

2. Mike put the tickets down and went to get ready. Sulley decided to sit in his chair and finish his cocoa. "I'll just have a quiet night in," he thought.

3. Later, Mike couldn't find the tickets. "Hey, Sulley, did you move the tickets as a joke?" giggled Mike. Sulley didn't know where they were, though.

4. Mike began to panic. "Celia will go crazy if I can't find them!" he cried. Sulley helped Mike to search their apartment, from top to bottom.

5. However, the tickets were nowhere to be found. "What will I tell Celia?" gulped Mike. "Just explain to her that you lost the tickets," said Sulley.

6. "She'll think I pretended to have the tickets, just to get her to come out with me," fretted Mike, as he set off. Sulley decided to go with him.

7. Celia was waiting outside the club. She frowned when she saw Mike's empty hands. "Where are the tickets?" she asked him. So Mike explained.

8. Luckily, just as they turned to leave, Celia spotted the lost tickets. "I must've put them on your chair!" giggled Mike, picking them off Sulley's back.

The end

Meet Mike!

Complete and then colour in this picture of Mike.

64

Growling groups

Can you spot which monster is the odd one out in each group?

1

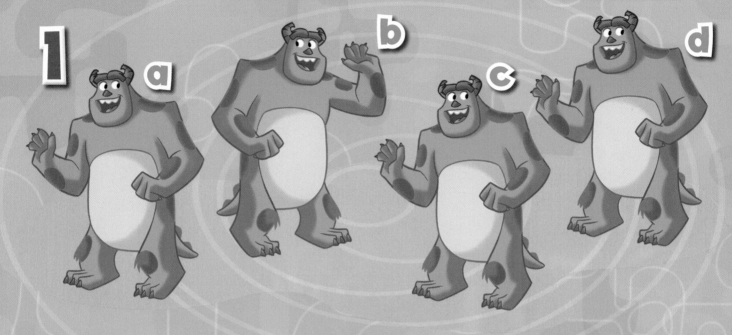

a

b

c

d

2

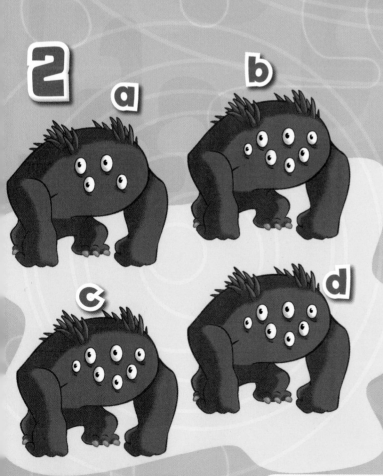

a

b

c

d

3

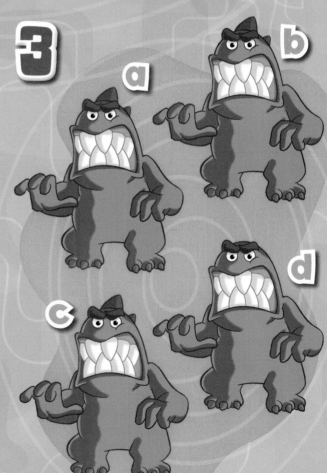

a

b

c

d

Answer: 1-b, 2-a, 3-d.

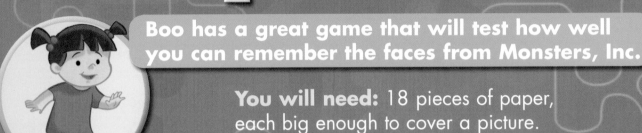

Snap and scare

Boo has a great game that will test how well you can remember the faces from Monsters, Inc.

You will need: 18 pieces of paper, each big enough to cover a picture.

How to play

Play this game with a friend. Both players should take a good look at the pictures and then cover them all with pieces of paper. Take it in turns to lift two pieces of paper, one from each page. If the pictures underneath match, the player keeps the pieces of paper and has another go. If the pictures don't match, the player replaces the pieces of paper and the next player has a go. The player with the most pieces of paper at the end is the winner!

A monster hug

Add some shocking colours, as Sulley hugs little Boo!

Have you seen the new Cars magazine?